DANGEROUS GAMES

DEADLY OCEAN

Sue Graves

RISING ★ STARS

Rising Stars UK Ltd.
7 Hatchers Mews, Bermondsey Street, London SE1 3GS
www.risingstars-uk.com

nasen

NASEN House, 4/5 Amber Business Village, Amber Close,
Amington, Tamworth, Staffordshire B77 4RP

Published 2009
Reprinted 2012 (twice), 2013

Cover design: pentacor**big**
Illustrations: Rob Lenihan, So Creative Ltd and Paul Loudon
Text design and typesetting: pentacor**big**
Publisher: Gill Budgell
Editorial project management: Lucy Poddington
Editorial consultant: Lorraine Petersen

British Library Cataloguing in Publication Data.
A CIP record for this book is available from the British Library.

ISBN: 978-1-84680-492-2

Printed by Craft Print International Limited, Singapore

CHAPTER 1

It had been a busy day in the office. Sima, Kojo and Tom were hot and tired. They all worked at Dangerous Games, a computer games company, and they were good mates.

They worked as a team. Sima was the designer. Kojo programmed the games and Tom tested them. They thought they had the best jobs ever.

"Let's chill out tonight," said Sima. She stretched her arms above her head. "I'm too hot and tired to do anything much. Why don't we go back to Kojo's and watch telly?"

"Good idea," said Kojo. "I'll make us some pasta, if you like."

"I've got a better idea," said Tom. He pointed to a website. "Look at this. A new Wave Rider centre is opening tonight in town. I've been to one before. You can surf all evening for a fiver. Let's go there. It'll cool us down."

"You're on!" said Kojo. "I've always wanted to try surfing."

Tom turned to Sima. "What about you, Sima? Are you up for it?"

Sima looked doubtful. "I've never done it before either," she said. Then she smiled. "But how hard can it be? Let's give it a go."

The Wave Rider centre was packed. Sima and
Kojo started at the lower end of the pool. The
waves weren't too big there. It was tricky at first
but they soon got better at it.

Then Kojo went to join Tom at the other end
of the pool. Tom was surfing the biggest waves
really well. But Kojo kept falling off.

At the end of the session, they all met up for a drink in the café.

"That was great!" said Sima. "Let's come here again."

"It's not as easy as it looks," said Kojo. "I thought those bigger waves were quite hard to surf."

"Rubbish!" said Tom. He yawned. "It was way too easy. I'd like to surf much harder waves than those. How about you make me a really difficult surfing game, Sima? Kojo can work his magic and we can test it for real like we've done before. Then I'll show you how good I really am."

"All right," said Sima. "You need taking down a peg or two! I'll draw up some designs tomorrow."

CHAPTER 2

The next day, Sima designed a surfing game. She gave it to Kojo to program. Tom was really keen to test it.

"What happens in the game?" he asked.

"You have to ride waves in the ocean," explained Sima. "The longer you ride a wave without falling off your board, the more points you get. You can win bonus points by doing difficult moves."

"Hey, that sounds brilliant," said Tom. "Can I try tube-riding? That's where you have the wave curling right over the top of you, so you're inside a tube of water. It's meant to be awesome."

"Well, I've designed the game on three levels," replied Sima. "You can choose how difficult you want the game to be. The first level is pretty easy, with small waves. The second level is harder, and the third is for the real experts."

"I can't wait to try it," said Tom eagerly.

By the end of the week the game was ready.

When everyone had left the office for the night, Tom, Sima and Kojo got ready to test the game for real.

"Remember, we must all touch the screen at the same time to enter the game," said Kojo. "It's over when we hear the words 'Game over'."

"OK," said Tom and Sima.

"I've programmed three levels, like you wanted, Sima," Kojo continued. "Which level shall we test tonight?"

"I think Level 2 would be best," said Sima. She clicked the button for Level 2.

They all put their hands on the screen.

"No!" yelled Tom suddenly. "Let's go for Level 3!"
He grabbed the mouse and clicked the button for
Level 3.

"Stop!" said Kojo. "You can't change levels just like
that. It could be dangerous!"

He tried to push Tom's hand away. But it was
too late. A bright light flashed, hurting their eyes.
They squeezed their eyes shut.

CHAPTER 3

When Tom, Kojo and Sima opened their eyes again, they were in a warm, crystal clear ocean. They could see a small tropical island not far away.

Three surfboards were floating nearby. They swam over to them and climbed aboard.

Kojo was really cross.

WHAT DID YOU DO THAT FOR, YOU IDIOT?

"Why did you change the level at the last minute? You might have made the game too dangerous," said Kojo.

Tom frowned. "What do you mean?" he asked.

"We pressed two different levels. That could corrupt the program. It could make the game lethal!" said Kojo.

Tom looked at the ocean and laughed.

"Come off it, Kojo," he said, pointing at the water. "The sea is as calm as a mill pond. I can't see any waves at all, let alone dangerous ones."

"Perhaps it will be OK," muttered Kojo, but he still felt cross with Tom.

Time went by and the sea stayed very calm. Tom began to get bored.

WHERE ARE THE WAVES? THIS IS GETTING REALLY BORING.

Suddenly Tom fell off his surfboard and disappeared under the surface of the water.

"What's happened?" panicked Sima. "Something's grabbed Tom and pulled him under!"

Sima and Kojo both dived underwater and surfaced a few seconds later. "I can't see him," yelled Sima.

"Me neither," said Kojo. Just then Tom's head bobbed up a short distance away. He was laughing.

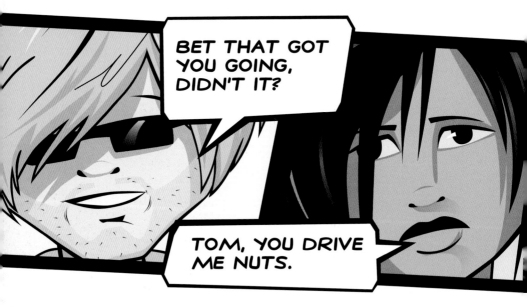

BET THAT GOT YOU GOING, DIDN'T IT?

TOM, YOU DRIVE ME NUTS.

Tom beckoned them over. "Come and look at this. There's an amazing underwater world down there."

They each took a deep breath and plunged underwater. A glittering coral reef teemed with life. Colourful fish darted in and out of the waving coral. A huge ray passed beneath them, its body rippling like a flag in a breeze.

"Well, it looks like the surfing game's not working, but this makes up for it," said Kojo when they were all at the surface again. "It's incredible."

Sima glanced towards the island. "Oh no!" she gasped. "This game isn't how I planned it at all. Look what's happening now!"

Sima, Tom and Kojo stared at the tropical island. The sea seemed to be draining away from it. It looked as if a giant plug had been pulled out of the seabed and all the water was disappearing down an invisible plughole.

Then the water around them began to shudder. They could feel themselves being dragged further and further out to sea. They clung onto their boards as they were pulled back through the water.

"What's happening?" screamed Sima.

"I think it's a tsunami," called Kojo. He looked scared.

"What?" shouted Tom.

"A giant wave!" said Kojo. "It's caused by an earthquake under the seabed."

WHAT'S GOING TO HAPPEN TO US?

The sea rose up behind them like a huge mountain. Then it rushed towards the island, taking the surfboards with it. But the wave didn't stop when it hit the shore. It washed over the island, crashing up the beach and smashing down trees. Sima shut her eyes tightly as her surfboard spun in the water.

The spinning stopped. Sima opened her eyes. She was lying on high ground near some rocks. She couldn't see Tom or Kojo anywhere. She opened her mouth to shout for help, but she couldn't make a sound. Her head hurt badly and she felt sick. Then everything went black.

Tom and Kojo managed to cling to some trees on the far side of the island. Neither of them was hurt except for some cuts and bruises. Sea water swirled around them, knee-deep and littered with broken branches.

"We made it," said Tom. "I thought we were all going to die." He looked around him. "Where's Sima?"

Kojo shook his head. "I've no idea. There's no sign of her. Let's hope she's on the island somewhere. Otherwise she might have drowned."

They waded through the water, calling her name.

Just then there was a bright light. A loud voice said "Game over!"

The bright light faded and Tom and Kojo found themselves back in the office.

CHAPTER 4

Tom and Kojo stared at each other.

"Sima's lost in the game world," said Tom. "What have I done?"

Kojo looked serious. Quickly, he reloaded the game. "She may be unconscious somewhere. Maybe that's why she didn't come back when the game ended. We must scan the game to see if we can spot her on the island," he said.

"But how can we get her back?" asked Tom. He was furious with himself for changing the game levels. He banged his fist down hard on the desk.

"Keep calm!" said Kojo. "Getting angry won't help Sima. Let's see if we can find her first. Then we'll think about what to do next."

Kojo and Tom checked the game carefully. Then Tom spotted something.

"Look," he said, "What's that near those rocks? Do you think it might be Sima?"

Kojo zoomed in on the rocks, but he couldn't make out what it was.

"I can't tell," said Kojo. "It could be a design fault. But let's hope it's Sima."

"How are we going to get her back to the real world?" asked Tom. "The game's over. We can't start a new one because different things might happen. We might lose Sima for ever."

Kojo thought hard. He did some calculations on a notepad.

"There *might* be something we can do," he said. "But it's very risky."

"I don't care how risky it is," said Tom. "We have to get Sima back. Do whatever it takes."

Kojo reprogrammed the game and put in a new set of instructions. It took a long time.

"I'm going to try and turn back the game clock," he explained. "That way, we might be able to re-enter the game and get Sima back before the time runs out."

"Good plan!" said Tom.

Kojo looked at the game clock on the screen.

"Oh no!" he said. "I can only turn the clock back five minutes. It might not be enough time to find her before the game finishes again."

"If that's all the time we've got, we must *make* it enough," said Tom. He looked at his watch. "I make it 7.22. Check?"

Kojo looked at his watch. "Check!" he said.

"Come on, let's go," said Tom.

They touched the screen together. Once again a bright light flashed. They shut their eyes.

When the light faded they were back on the island.

CHAPTER 5

The tsunami had wrecked the island. Most of it was still flooded. Kojo pointed to the higher ground which rose above the muddy water.

LOOK, THE ROCKS ARE UP THERE. THAT'S WHERE SIMA MIGHT BE.

THEN LET'S GET THERE FAST. COME ON. WE'VE NO TIME TO LOSE.

They waded to the dry land and climbed up through the trees. Kojo looked at his watch. There were only two minutes of the game left.

They ran towards the rocks, calling Sima's name. But everywhere was silent.

Tom stood still. He checked his watch. Now there was only a minute left. It was hopeless.

Just then Tom heard something move behind the bushes. There was a groaning sound. He pushed the bushes aside. Sima was lying in the long grass. She had a deep cut on her head. Tom picked her up and held her close to him.

Kojo came running over.

They heard the loud voice again, saying "Game over". There was a bright light. They all shut their eyes.

The next thing they knew they were back in the office.

Tom held Sima tightly.

"I thought we'd lost you for ever," he said seriously.
He looked at the cut on her head. "You're hurt.
What can I do to make you feel better?"

Sima smiled. "You can put me down for a start!"

Tom laughed as he carefully put her down.
"That's a relief," he said. "My arms were about
to drop off. I'm not cut out for weightlifting!"

"You're *sooo* not funny!" said Sima and she rolled
her eyes.

Glossary of terms

coral reef a ridge in the sea, made up of tiny living creatures

corrupt to damage a computer program

designer a person who plans how something will work and how it will look

lethal deadly

program to write a computer game or other computer program

ray a kind of fish which has a flat body and wing-like fins

seabed the ocean floor

tropical places which are in the hottest parts of the world

tsunami a giant wave, often caused by an earthquake under the seabed

unconscious in a faint

Quiz

1 What did Kojo offer to cook for Tom and Sima?

2 What was the name of the centre where Sima, Tom and Kojo went surfing?

3 How many levels did the new computer game have?

4 Which level did Sima want to test?

5 Which level did Tom want to play?

6 What sort of island was in the game?

7 What was the name of the giant wave?

8 Who got left behind on the island?

9 What did Kojo do to make it possible to go back into the game?

10 How long did Tom and Kojo have to find Sima?

ABOUT THE AUTHOR

Sue Graves has taught for thirty years in Cheshire schools. She has been writing for more than ten years and has written well over a hundred books for children and young adults.

"Nearly everyone loves computer games. They are popular with all age groups — especially young adults. But I've often thought it would be amazing to play a computer game for real. To be in on the action would be the best experience ever! That's why I wrote these stories. I hope you enjoy reading them as much as I've enjoyed writing them for you."

ANSWERS TO QUIZ

1   Pasta

2   Wave Rider centre

3   Three

4   Two

5   Three

6   Tropical

7   Tsunami

8   Sima

9   He turned back the game clock

10   Five minutes